In-App Purchases

Both Fortnite Save The World and Fortnite Battle Royale contain in-app purchases, which are covered throughout this book, so please be sure to seek approval from a parent/ grown-up or the bill payer before purchasing any additional add-ons, including Battle Passes, V-Bucks and character/ weapon skins.

LB BOOKS

Little Brother Books Ltd, Ground Floor, 23 Southernhay East, Exeter, Devon, EX1 1QL
books@littlebrotherbooks.co.uk
www.littlebrotherbooks.co.uk
The Little Brother Books trademarks, logos, email, and website addresses are sole and exclusive properties of Little Brother Books Limited.
Published 2024. Printed in China.
Little Brother Books, 77 Camden Street Lower, Dublin DO2 XE80.

CHALLENGE CORNER!

Can you prove yourself to be a truly elite Fortnite fan by solving this fiendish crossword and defeating the dastardly wordsearch?

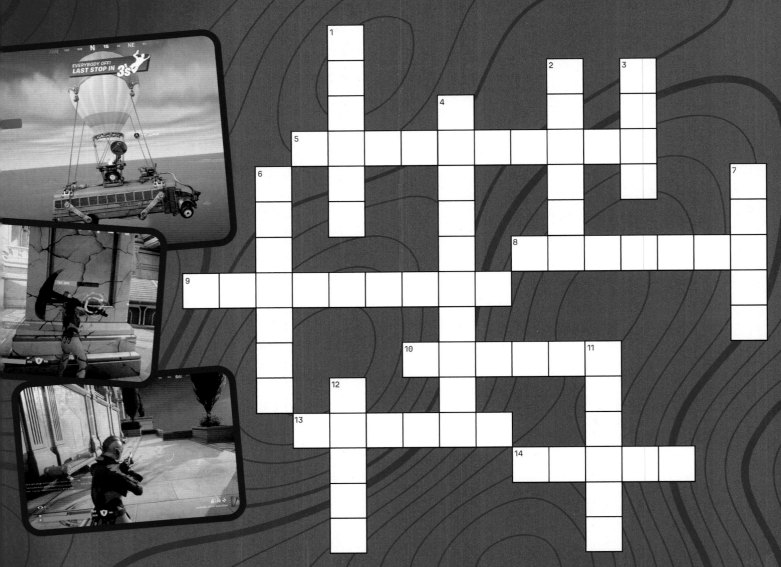

Across

5) Another name for the act of gathering materials (10).
8) An explosive weapon type that can be thrown at opponents (7).
9) The name of the vehicle you jump from at the start of the game ((6,3).
10) The in-game currency you can use to buy skins and other goodies! (1,5).
13) A piece of equipment that helps you land safely on The Island (6).
14) A furry animal that conceals goodies in the game (5).

Down

1) Victory _____, the name given to a win in the game (6).
2) _____ rifle, an ideal weapon for long-range shots (6).
3) A popular brick-based lego gamer that has now joined the Fortnite world! (4).
4) A large multiplayer game mode (4,6).
6) A weapon type that is excellent when used at close range (7).
7) A hollow wooden container that contains loot in Fortnite (5).
11) The name for a four-player team mode (6).
12) The blue ooze found on The Island that provides health benefits when consumed (5).

Answers on page 78.

4

WORDSEARCH

L	U	G	S	X	T	R	I	O	S	O	S	H	C
A	N	B	A	N	D	A	G	E	S	R	A	M	T
C	C	E	M	O	T	E	S	M	R	O	T	S	G
I	O	L	E	G	E	N	D	A	R	Y	I	I	L
E	M	I	U	E	E	G	N	E	L	L	A	H	C
H	M	P	S	U	X	T	H	S	E	S	H	B	C
R	O	C	K	E	T	A	U	S	H	P	S	C	S
N	N	D	A	S	N	B	K	I	E	C	O	K	L
E	X	G	A	R	E	O	E	C	S	E	P	I	C
O	D	D	B	L	O	L	R	N	I	R	I	S	N
T	I	E	T	I	D	E	I	R	S	P	I	N	O
M	M	T	E	U	I	K	N	O	I	T	O	P	M
S	A	U	G	E	S	M	K	T	S	L	P	S	O
B	A	C	K	B	L	I	N	G	O	C	E	E	A

Words to find:

- ☐ CHALLENGE
- ☐ MIDAS
- ☐ ROCKET
- ☐ PICKAXE
- ☐ EMOTES
- ☐ TRIOS
- ☐ BANDAGES
- ☐ POTION
- ☐ SHIELD
- ☐ EPIC
- ☐ LEGENDARY
- ☐ UNCOMMON
- ☐ STORM
- ☐ SKINS
- ☐ BATTLE BUS
- ☐ BACK BLING

Answers on page 78.

AMAZING AVATARS

We asked you to share your favourite skins with us, perhaps combined with your favourite back bling – and hundreds of you got in touch! Thanks to everyone who sent us an image – here are some of our favourites! Who do you think looks the coolest going into battle?

Ricardo, 11

Who! Looks like Spiderman has had a bit of a falling out with Venom! Is Venom taking control?

Harry, 11

We love this idea, sending The Brat into combat with the motorised Renegade Rustcat back bling. Can anyone smell burnt hotdog?

Austin, 10

Excuse us, but we think this banana is past its best before date! Not only is it full of bones, it's also grown wings!

Hadley, 8

Woof woof! The Brat carrying Brian from Family Guy makes for a double dog adventure!

Blake, 9

Hot hot hot! We love the brightness of this daring combo – you'd better keep moving if you decide to use it yourself!

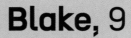

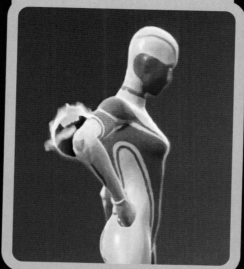

Mark, 10

How can Sypher get any cooler, we hear you ask? Well, by pairing him with some awesome back bling, of course!

Logan, 8

What's scarier than Oscar the tiger? Oscar the tiger with the Diselback back bling! There's no outrunning this predator!

Josh, 12

This combo gives us two legends for the price of one! MrBeast of internet superfame, along with Fortnite's own icon Peely as backbling!

Joseph, 15

As if Kimiko Five-Tails wasn't enough of a threat, she gets even more dangerous when you add wings!

Charilaos, 10

Spectra Knight's pulsating suit of armour has to be one of the most terrifying sights in Fortnite!

Tommy, 9

You have to hand it to Ruby, she even has a style that allows her to rep Fortnite — while she is IN Fortnite!

Reuben, 10

The perfect outfit for Easter, this bunny even has somewhere to stash all his eggs!

Dylan, 12

Purradise Meowicles could not be MORE beach ready than he is here, with all of his accessories perfect for topping up his tan!

Jack, 14

Another knight-themed skin, the stunning effects on Galaxy Knight's skin makes this choice out of this world!

Mia, 10

Kado Thorne's black and white look is perfect for skulking in the shadows while also looking absolutely cool!

Seán, 11

This cuddly combo looks like it's ready to snuggle up and be tucked into bed – but don't be fooled, on the Island everyone is an opponent!

Adam, 9

As winter draws in, you'll need to be ready to look good on the slopes and this bright Subzero Cryptic skin certainly fits the bill!

Eli, 8

Fortnite might be a very modern game, but it can take inspiration from the oldest stories – such as this depiction of Medusa from Greek mythology!

Miles, 7

Pay homage to the crazy Peter Griffin, looking resplendent here in a gold outfit! Throw in an automobile back bling for even more awesome!

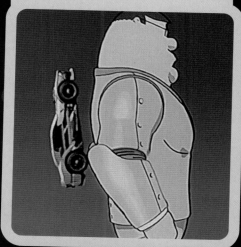

William, 9

Fortnite might be one of the latest titles on the gaming block, but this skin pays homage to Doom, one of the older members of the gaming community!

TOP TEN FUN CHALLENGES!

Fortnite is loads of fun as it is, but we've looked at the different ways some players add an extra challenge into the mix. If you'd like to try something extra with your Fortnite experience, then we've ranked ten of our favourite ways to play. Join us as we count down to our number one – what's yours?

10

The no-look challenge

Disable all your HUD options in the settings menu and try to win a match without visual aids such as the minimap, your health bar or how much ammo you have left!

The shotgun challenge

Try to win a game using only shotguns – nothing else is allowed! You'll need to avoid ranged combat altogether!

9

8

The no-healing challenge

Play a match without using any healing items at all, meaning you can only rely on your starting health levels.

The solo squad challenge

Play squads match (or duos or trios if you want a lesser challenge) on no fill. You'll be a team of one, playing alone against everyone else working in groups!

7

6 The sniper challenge

Win a match using only sniper rifles. This is the opposite of the shotgun challenge – you'll be deadly at distance but in big trouble up close!

5 The skybase challenge

Build a base and try to win the game staying only within your base. You can move as the storm closes in, but only to build another base that you must then stay inside!

The throwing challenge

You can only use thrown weapons such as grenades and impulse grenades to secure a Victory Royale!

4

3 The no-build challenge

Win a game without building anything. This obviously does not count if you are playing Zero Build – you need to do it in Battle Royale!

The melee challenge

You can only use melee weapons in this challenge. That includes your harvesting tools, as well as any other hand-to-hand weapons available in the game!

2

1 The pacifist challenge

Win a game without any eliminations! You'll need to focus on stealth and avoiding combat to pull this one off!

MASTER YOUR SETTINGS

The settings used by the best Fortnite players are crucial to gaining an edge over their opponents. We have spent countless hours testing and adjusting the settings to bring you our recommendations on how they can aid in improving your gameplay.

Sound settings

Sound is crucial in Fortnite! Knowing where opponents are coming from and where the danger is can make the difference between a Victory Royale and an early trip back to the lobby.

In the sound settings, we suggest setting sound effects to 100%. For multiplayer modes, it's recommended to set voice chat between 80% and 100% depending on personal preference to be able to hear teammates.

We always turn music, dialogue and cinematics to lower sound settings. This means characters in the game chatting away or incidental music effects won't mask the sound of anything more important — like approaching opponents!

Visualise sound effects

In the sound section of settings, we always turn 'Visualise Sound Effects' to ON.

- Any noise above a certain level appears on the heads-up display.
- It makes it much quicker to see where gunfire is coming from.
- Footprints will appear, indicating someone walking or running nearby.

Not all sounds will appear! In particular, players moving while crouching will not make sound loud enough to appear on the display — but those can still be heard through speakers or headphones if those volume settings are right!

Gameplay settings

HUD scale

This controls the size of the HUD (Heads-up display). The screen displays the mini-map, how much of each material is being carried, current level, health and shield. Shrinking it provides a better view of the action – but too small can make it hard to keep track of that important information! We think that 70% is a good compromise – check out our experiment!

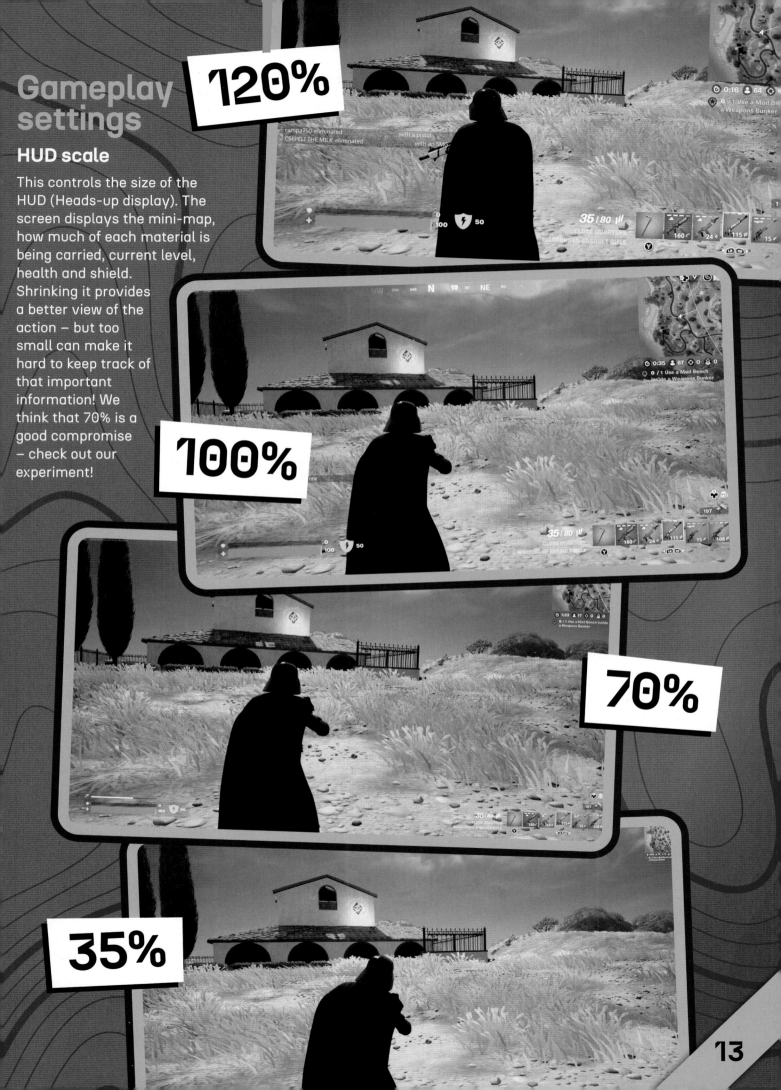

120%

100%

70%

35%

Autosort items

In the game section of settings, selecting Preferred Item Slots means the player can decide which slots certain weapons and consumables will automatically be assigned to.

This is an absolutely essential pro tip – all of the top players have this turned on. It sounds like a small detail but by having certain weapons types in the same slots all the time, the best players find they can instinctively switch between them – for example, a shotgun in slot 1, an assault rifle in slot 2 and a sniper rifle in slot 3.

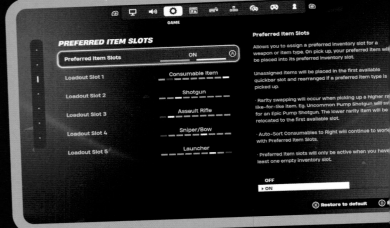

Opening doors

In the game section of your settings, we advise turning Auto Open Doors OFF, otherwise you'll automatically open any door you are close to. It sounds like it would save time but it will often mean you'll open doors when you'd rather avoid detection! Keep it turned off! Don't be tempted!

Faster looting!

In the game section of settings, turn Tap to Search/Interact to ON. This will allow players to open chests and interact with items with a single button press instead of holding it down for a couple of seconds. Again, it's a small change but it saves a tiny fraction in allowing the player to be ready to move again – those little details really matter!

Preset options

As well as the specific alterations we've explored here, you can also choose broader 'gaming styles' based on your natural play style. These assign your controls in a way best suited to the corresponding gamer type. You'll find these options in the Controller Mapping section of your settings, under Presets. If you want to explore your own gaming style, we suggest using the presets as a starting point and adding your own changes.

The basic gamer types available are:
- Old School
- Quick Builder
- Combat Pro
- Builder Pro

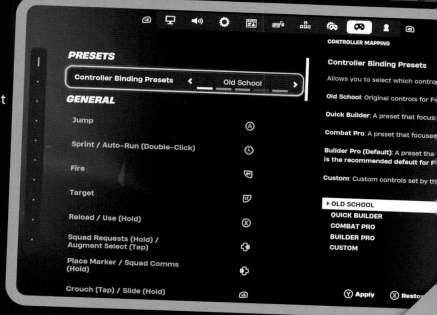

THE RAMP PUSH

THE PROBLEM: You are facing an opponent on the other side of a large open area. You don't have a long range weapon and your opponent is between you and safety. You need to move towards him, but you don't want to give him an easy shot.

OUR SOLUTION: This is the ideal scenario for the ramp push. This involves you charging towards your opponent, using a series of small ramps to provide you with cover AND a raised shooting position.

Step 2

Use wood if you have plenty. Your builds will be temporary, and only need to last a few seconds each – you're looking for speed of build and movement rather than durability, so wood is definitely your friend here.

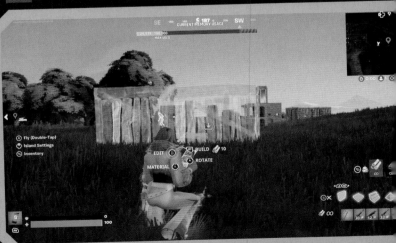

Step 1

Make sure you have a decent fix on your opponent's position so you know where they are. This will enable you to make sure you are moving in the right direction – you don't want to get caught out attacking the wrong location.

Step 3

Place a single 'wall' piece in front of you (but not too close – you need a gap for the next step!). The wall piece is just to protect the ramp you're about to build so it isn't destroyed immediately.

Step 4

Now add a ramp leading up to the wall you've just built. Run up the ramp, using the height advantage to take a shot or two at your opponent before you drop off the ramp into open space.

Step 5

Repeat the process. With each interaction of your ramp, you'll be moving closer to your opponent and you should be able to land a couple of hits on them each time.

Step 6

If your opponent is still in one piece as you close in on their location, switch to a shotgun

FORTNITE BASICS

Whatever game mode you're playing, you need to know what you're doing. Here at GamesWarrior, we've checked out hundreds of different tactics that can help secure a Victory Royale — here are the ones we found to be the most effective!

Right tool for the job

Winning gamers use the right weapon for the right situation. Shotguns are pointless at distance, while there's no point in carrying a sniper rifle inside a building.

GAMESWARRIOR'S VERDICT

Having the right weapon ready to go avoids wasting time switching weapons when the action starts!

One in the chamber

All the top players reload after every skirmish, or when picking up weapons that their opponents have used! Otherwise, they could run out of ammo after a single shot in their next battle, which could be the difference between winning and losing.

GAMESWARRIOR'S VERDICT

Make it a regular habit to reload frequently — including cycling through ALL your weapons to check they are fully loaded and ready to go!

Pick up everything

It is surprising how few players pick up all the weapons they find when they first land until their inventory is full, even if the weapons are rubbish and don't suit them.

GAMESWARRIOR'S VERDICT

Picking up weapons is a great way to make sure you don't get picked off by someone who dropped just behind you! When you find better weapons, just switch to them immediately!

Leave nothing behind!

Pro players never leave anything useful behind that their opponents could use to their benefit. Even though these items may not be of much use, they make sure the next visitor to the area won't be getting much from the experience!

GAMESWARRIOR'S VERDICT

It's a brilliant tactic to smash barrels, destroy vending machines, light campfires and generally leave as little as possible behind for your rivals to use!

Don't fear the early storm

Many skilled Fortnite players use the storm as cover in the early stages of a game, as it only inflicts minor damage – one HP per second. Sometimes, they'll even head back into the storm to pick up valuable loot.

GAMESWARRIOR'S VERDICT

Always know how much damage the storm will do to you if it catches you, and don't risk sprinting into danger just to avoid a minimal loss of health.

Watch the storm

It is easy to get distracted in combat. Top players keep their concentration to avoid having to sprint from the storm and making themselves an easy target for their rivals. This is particularly important late in the game, where the storm can do significant damage.

GAMESWARRIOR'S VERDICT

You should always know where the storm is, where you need to move to, and how much time you have to get there. Don't get distracted!

Disguise your presence

Players who are stealthy ensure they don't leave any clues that could lead opponents to their hiding place. They keep their presence hidden from opponents to give themselves the edge in combat.

GAMESWARRIOR'S VERDICT

Closing doors and parking cars away from buildings you want to hide in makes it harder for opponents to know where you are when they arrive at your location.

19

Look out for signs

Other players might not be as careful as you! They may leave clues behind – opened doors, battle damage to buildings and looted chests will tell you if someone has been to an area before you arrived!

GAMESWARRIOR'S VERDICT

It's best to exercise extra caution if there are signs of previous activity at a location – but it's best to be careful anyway in case an opponent is lying in wait!

Money makes the world go round

Gold can be a big help in Fortnite, from hiring an assistant to paying for weapons and heals from the vending machines on The Island. Accepting bounties and challenges whenever they appear is a great way to earn more gold to spend on extras when they are badly needed.

GAMESWARRIOR'S VERDICT

There's no penalty for not pursuing a side quest or failing to achieve it, so we think it always makes sense to accept them!

A helping hand

In Solos, hiring a character on the Island can provide you with a significant advantage. If you have enough gold, having an extra set of hands can bring many benefits – not least of all distracting opponents who attack you by presenting them with two targets returning fire instead of just one.

GAMESWARRIOR'S VERDICT

We think it's a brilliant tactic to use a hired character to enter buildings first, to determine whether an opponent is waiting inside!

Gather more gold

As well as earning gold through challenges, it can be found on the Island itself. Shop tills glow gold to indicate they have gold inside, and opening them reveals their golden contents! A smart way to make money is to use EMP devices near to vending machines, which will throw out gold each time they are hit!

GAMESWARRIOR'S VERDICT

Money makes the world go round, so maximising any opportunity to gather more gold makes complete sense!

Build quickly under fire

When watching the top players, you'll notice that building is second nature to them. When they come under fire, they will often build an L shaped wall with the angle pointing in the general direction of the shot. The cover this provides can buy vital seconds while they decide what to do next!

Sneak a peek

The camera angle is positioned high and behind the player's avatar, allowing them to see around corners and over obstacles to locate opponents without having to step out from cover!

Harvesting materials

Harvesting materials early in the game is a popular tactic with players who like to build cover, as there's less chance of encountering other players. Many people harvest from internal walls to gather materials without exposing themselves to long-range attacks.

Smart tagging

Loot can be tagged from distance, which is a useful strategy to identify what something is without having to approach it physically. This tactic doesn't even need a scope on a weapon to pull off, although having one would make it easier.

GAMESWARRIOR'S VERDICT

Successfully highlighting an item of loot will make an icon representing it appear on the screen, making it easier to decide whether it is worth the risk of breaking cover to collect it or not.

Learn the map

There's no substitute for knowing the map properly. Practise makes perfect and successful players put the hours in so they know what they are likely to encounter and where – bushes, buildings, vehicles and so on...

GAMESWARRIOR'S VERDICT

Knowing the map can help you navigate towards the storm circle safely, helping you avoid likely hot spots and making sure you know where you can find loot.

Drop wisely

Players that stick to two or three drop zones will usually get off to better starts than those who drop in random places each time, because they'll know their landing location inside out before long. It can make getting off to a good start much easier.

GAMESWARRIOR'S VERDICT

Explore locations that are a little off the beaten track – it's a great way to find places that are home to a good amount of loot but won't have loads of opponents dropping in too.

See how it's done

Watching the top pros on streaming services is a great way to pick up their secrets for yourself and can help you improve your own game. Similarly, it makes sense to keep watching any players who eliminate you in awe-inspiring ways, rather than rushing back to the lobby to play again.

GAMESWARRIOR'S VERDICT

Watching other players and exploring areas of the map that you might not normally visit are great ways to learn new tactics and techniques.

Equip yourself well

For a player to be ready for any situation, they will need to carry a close-range, mid-range and long-range weapon at all times. This covers all eventualities and means however they are attacked, they can retaliate.

GAMESWARRIOR'S VERDICT

A balanced payload is preferable to picking up lots of similar weapons, which can limit your options in battle.

Master the shotgun

Close combat is an essential skill that all the top players excel at, especially towards the latter stages. Mastering the use of the shotgun is crucial – without it, it is very hard to succeed.

GAMESWARRIOR'S VERDICT

Spend some time getting the hang of whichever shotguns are available in the game – you won't regret it.

Build to heal

Players are vulnerable when healing – they can't really move much, and obviously aren't maxed out on health and shields. A popular tactic to stay safe is known as 'turtling' – building four walls and a roof to create a little hut and healing inside it safe from sniper scopes!

GAMESWARRIOR'S VERDICT

Turtling is absolutely the best approach if you need to heal and there are no buildings nearby – mastering it is a must!

Edit your builds

Building is an important skill, but editing takes it to the next level. You'll see the better players in the game regularly edit a window into a wall, fire, then edit the window back out again!

GAMESWARRIOR'S VERDICT

It takes practise, but editing your own builds quickly can make the difference between winning and losing in the final few battles.

Know your weapons

It's easy to drop an uncommon weapon in favour of a rare version of a different but similar type of weapon (different assault rifles, for example). However, sometimes, seemingly 'weaker' weapons can do more damage than 'stronger' alternatives.

GAMESWARRIOR'S VERDICT

There's no substitute for learning how powerful different weapons are – if it's too hard to remember, they can always be double checked in the inventory.

The gift of fire

When players have taken cover in wooden builds, it can be hard to eliminate them. A smart tactic involves using weapons that cause fire – such as grenades, or exploding petrol containers. The flames will force the hiding player to flee, leaving them vulnerable to attack.

GAMESWARRIOR'S VERDICT

Thinking laterally and using flames to damage concealed opponents or flush them out of their hiding places is a brilliant way to defeat opponents who are expert builders.

Don't stop moving

Staying still is dangerous, which is why skilled players are always on the move (unless they are trying to hide). They zig zag when running, they jump at unpredictable moments and switch between standing and crouching – they do everything possible to make it harder to hit them.

GAMESWARRIOR'S VERDICT

Avoid being a stationary target at all costs. Moving in unpredictable ways when travelling between locations can convince opponents not to even take a shot – and if they do fire, it makes their chances of scoring a decisive hit much lower.

Pick your battles

The best players may be despatching opponents left right and centre from the moment they land, but that's not always an achievable tactic for us mere mortals. Carefully selecting when to engage with opponents and when to stay out of trouble is a key part of reaching the later rounds of a Battle Royale.

GAMESWARRIOR'S VERDICT

Speculative potshots from distance can often attract unwanted attention and bring more trouble than they are worth. We recommend only engaging when you can be sure that you have the upper hand and the element of surprise!

MULTIPLAYER BASICS

Things get frantic when you hook up with your crew to seek out a Victory Royale! No man is an island – even ON the Island! We've explored some of the most successful multiplayer tactics out there and after hours of painstaking research (and a whole lot of eliminations!) we can bring you our verdict on the best ways to secure a win!

Communicate

In Fortnite, the best players in team-based games are the strongest communicators. They'll call out enemy positions, loot locations, and storm movement so that their squad runs like a well-oiled machine. We think that sharing plans and strategies leads to smarter rotations and coordinated attacks. Teamwork triumphs in Fortnite, and that teamwork thrives on talking it out.

GW RATING ★★★★☆

Look the same

An increasingly popular – and smart – tactic in multiplayer modes is for a whole squad to wear the same skins. Enemies become unsure who to target in a flurry of matching jumpsuits, while spotting teammates becomes a breeze amidst the chaos. We're definitely on board with this tactic, looking cool is great, but blending into your surroundings is even better.

GW RATING ★★★★☆

26

Look out for each other

When you watch the best players play in teams, you can see that they forget all about lone wolf glory. Covering your teammates is the lifeblood of victory. We suggest that a squad works best if someone is always offering cover – looking out for opponents while the others harvest or build, for example. Remember, you're not just teammates, you're each other's eyes and ears out there.

GW RATING ★★★★★

Share the wealth

Good teams know that sharing is the ultimate survival tactic. We recommend taking that on board, and that you share heals, shields, and ammo – a well-equipped squad is a force to be reckoned with. Try to play to each other's strengths too – hand over that gold sniper rifle to your buddy who is more accurate than you are. Remember, you win together, so loot together!

GW RATING ★★★★★

Practise makes perfect

When you watch streamers playing in squads and racking up the wins like they are going out of fashion, you should know that isn't happening by accident. Playing together with the same crew over and over means everyone knows how each other plays – and that's a tactic we think you should be bringing to your own multiplayer games!

GW RATING ★★★★★

Watch and learn

We spend a lot of time watching streamers to assess how good their tactics are, as well as figuring out our own approach. We think it's a great way to see the latest thinking in the game and find innovative solutions to new challenges that a game like Fortnite throws up from time to time.

Split your heals

In Fortnite squads, top players know that victory hinges on health. A teammate down is a teammate out. Sharing heals isn't charity, it's strategy. A quick bandage or medkit can turn a losing fight, and reviving a downed friend with a shared shield can snatch victory from the jaws of defeat. We say it's essential to remember, you're only as strong as your weakest teammate, so spread the health around!

Careful when reviving or rebooting

Reviving teammates is essential, but it's not something that the best players prioritise unless it is safe to do so. Sometimes it is safer to collect a reboot card when the battle is over rather than trying to revive a downed colleague, so we say choose your moment wisely. If you are playing with more than two players, then some of the group should cover the player carrying out the revival or reboot as well – and if you can, build some defences first for safety!

Finish the job

In Fortnite squads, eliminating a downed player secures several advantages. It prevents them from calling out your position or being revived later, and they might drop valuable loot as well. However, we would urge caution, and only finish downed players off if it is safe to do so. Focus on remaining enemies first if they pose an immediate threat.

Focus fire

Organised, focused teams are the most likely winners on Fortnite, and one way to emulate them is to try and focus your squad's fire on the same member of an opposing group. If you all hit the same player and get them eliminated from the skirmish quickly, the odds will tilt in your favour!

Hire a helper

Hiring an NPC in squads adds an extra fighter, boosting your firepower. Some NPCs offer unique perks like scouting for enemies or throwing down heals. They can also distract opponents or take down a weakened opponent on your behalf. However, hiring them is a tactic that not many players embrace (especially in squads). We think you should buck that trend and add an NPC to your roster when the chance presents itself. They can also be used to revive you during a gunfight, leaving your teammates free to focus on battling back against your opponents!

THE QUICK BUILD

THE PROBLEM:
When playing Battle Royale, coming under fire while in the open puts you at real risk of an early exit. With nowhere to hide and without a clear shot at your rival, you need to find a way to stay safe – and quickly!

OUR SOLUTION:
Learning to build quickly is essential in standard Battle Royale, and practising a quick-build technique over and over is a great idea. You'll soon find yourself able to construct a structure quickly to keep yourself safe and buy time to return fire.

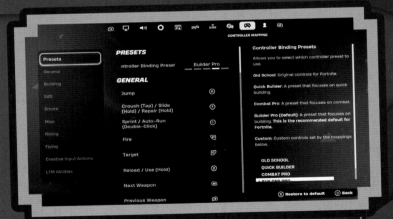

Step 2

It's not wise to wait until you are under fire to think about building materials! One approach is to collect materials early in the game so that you're ready for combat later on – there's less chance of being ambushed while harvesting if you do it early.

Step 1

Being able to build under pressure starts with having access to the right tools quickly. A preferred option is to use the Builder Pro preset controls, but you might find another configuration easier – speed is key, and being able to access different shaped pieces rapidly should be your main focus.

Step 3

As soon as gunfire rings out and you're exposed, build an L-shaped wall with the corner pointing in the general direction where the shots are coming from. Build two units high to ensure you still have decent cover even if your opponent is shooting from an elevated position.

Step 4

The gunfire may attract other players keen to finish you off while you are engaged in combat, so don't forget to cover your own back! Quickly spin and build a few walls behind you just as a precaution!

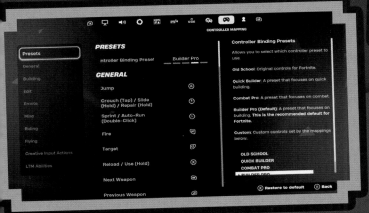

Step 5

It's time to face up to your opponent! Build a ramp up to the top of the L-shaped walls you initially constructed, and climb it. From the top, you should now be able to return fire at your would-be assassin!

Step 6

Even the most skilled players take damage, and it's likely you will too! Remember to keep an eye on your shields and health and if you take a few hits, retreat to the safety of your build while you heal up!

GAMESWARRIOR'S VERDICT

This is one of the essential techniques to master. Learning how to build quickly and return fire will turn certain eliminations into potential Victory Royales.

GW RATING ★★★★☆

TEAM RUMBLE BASICS

Team Rumble is a fast and furious mode where it can be hard to know what's going on! We've dedicated many hours to watching how the top players come out on top time after time, so here's our take on some of the tactics being used out there!

← Build up to bossing it!

It might feel very tempting to rush into the middle of combat as soon as the bullets start flying, and you'll see plenty of players doing exactly that and seeming to thrive on it. However, we advise taking your time and building your skill levels up before trying that approach!

Team Rumble is a very different dynamic to Battle Royale mode, and it takes a little getting used to. We advise sticking to the edges of the battles while you find your feet and increase your confidence, then moving to the middle of the battle when you feel ready!

Heal quickly →

The action is fast and furious in Team Rumble, and the odds of players getting a few seconds to themselves are pretty long. That's why the top players don't tend to bother with 'slow' heals such as MedKits or Big Pots. Instead, they prioritise 'fast' heals including Chug Splashes.

We recommend following their lead – it's highly unlikely you'll have enough time to administer a MedKit without coming under attack so you may as well prioritise faster ways to heal – and ideally ones that will heal any nearby teammates too!

↑ Choose your equipment wisely!

Once the storm circle shrinks to put both teams in combat with each other, it becomes much harder to find weapons. Eliminations in Team Rumble do not mean a loss of weapons, so any weapons found early in the game are likely to form the backbone of a player's tactics.

For that reason, better players will devote time to searching for the best possible inventory before joining

the battle. We recommend landing in areas with lots of chests and loot, and opening as many as you can until you have a good range of weapons in your inventory. Once the bullets start flying and the storm circle is shrinking and moving, there'll be no time to improve it – so get it right from the start!

→ Don't go rogue!

Although it's a large-sided game, the more successful players tend to be those who stick close to their team, rather than going rogue and heading off alone. Solo players trying to flank opponents or work alone will be picked off quickly, but by staying close to the rest of the team, there is safety in numbers.

That's why it's a good tactic to stick close to the rest of your team – they will be able to help you if you are attacked and instead of you being eliminated, it could be your assailant that ends up needing to respawn!

TOP TEN COLLABS

Fortnite has absorbed some of the biggest brands in the world as collaborations, and each one has added a little something to the Fortnite universe! Here's our top ten collaborations, in the order we love them. Do you agree with our ranking? What's your favourite Fortnite collab?

10 Marshmello

Fortnite's first musical crossover experience saw gamer and Fortnite fan Marshmello holding an in-game concert at Pleasant Park. The event, held back in 2019, was attended by a staggering 10.7 million fans who were treated to an exclusive set from the celebrated DJ.

Rick and Morty 9

This iconic pair of interdimensional travellers appeared in Fortnite in August 2022. With Fortnite having a backstory that's all about alternative realities, their appearance was hardly unexpected – and their skins and back bling have reappeared in the Item Shop a few times since too!

8 Streaming Legends

Fortnite has always been about its community, but Epic took that a stage further with the inspired decision to create skins based on some of the biggest streamers whose support helped the game become the behemoth it has become! The likes of Ninja, Lazerbeam and Ali-A are now IN the game they became famous for playing!

Ninja Turtles 7

Leonardo, Michelangelo, Donatello and Raphael figured that the best way to promote their new movies was to pop up in Fortnite! The ooze-tastic foursome (perfect for playing Squads!) were later joined by Shredder, while Kevin Eastman, the co-creator of TMNT, even contributed loading screen art!

6 Travis Scott

Marshmello got the music theme rolling in Fortnite, but Travis Scott took it to the next level in 2020 with his 'Astronomical' event that was more an immersive experience than a concert. The event was so popular it was held across five screenings over two days, with almost 28 million people joining in!

5 Family Guy

Most of the brands that cross over into Fortnite have a similar family-friendly feel to Epic's masterpiece – but not the distinctly adult Peter Griffin! His hilariously huge avatar was a Battle Pass reward, along with the rest of the gang – even Brian the dog and the giant chicken!

Dragonball Z

A legendary gaming franchise, Dragonball Z was a huge success when it landed in Fortnite in August 2022. It was a limited time event, and as well as featuring skins for characters such as Goku and San Gohan, it also incorporated legendary items such as the Nimbus Cloud and the Kamehameha energy blast!

3 Ariana Grande

If there was a sign that Fortnite was truly a mainstream experience, it came when Ariana Grande announced a collab. The pocket-sized pop star performed five concerts over three days, attracting 27 million gamers to her in-game gigs – with an Ariana skin occasionally appearing in the Item Shop ever since!

Marvel

The MCU is a franchising giant, and it has steamrollered its way onto the Island many times over! Way back in 2019, the Avengers formed part of the Fortnite storyline to promote Avengers: Endgame and since then Iron Man, Captain America, Spiderman and the crew have been regular visitors!

1 Star Wars

Our favourite collab has to be Star Wars – not only have LOADS of characters been ported across as skins, but Fortnite hosts Star Wars-themed content every year around Star Wars day (May 4th). As well as the skins, getting hands-on with blasters and lightsabers is pretty cool too!

Guide to ROCKET RACING

After the success of Rocket League, Rocket Racing landed in Fortnite to offer another brilliant gaming experience — this time based on racing other players round a track. Here's the GamesWarrior way to make sure you're in pole position when it comes to claiming a place on the podium!

← Off to a flier

A great race has to get off to a great start, so the most successful players are almost always those who are able to get out in front early on. Races start with three red lights that count down to a green light — any player that hits their accelerator before the light turns green will be at an immediate disadvantage! The quicker the accelerator is hit AFTER the light goes green the quicker the start will be! It's a vital technique to master!

Drifting away →

Drifting fills up the speed boost bar, which means greater speeds can be achieved much more often. Drifting round corners is a key technique to master, but the very fastest players will also perform 'mini-drifts' while racing on straight sections to build their boost meter even quicker.

← Use your turbo wisely

When that turbo meter is full, it turns white and an on-screen prompt appears urging you to activate it. However, it is a smarter tactic to delay using the boost so that it can be deployed at a point where it really can have an impact. You won't find top players hitting their speed boosts through bendy sections of track where they'll need to brake — they save it for the straight sections where they can go faster!

→ Learn the maps!

There's no substitute for getting to know each circuit inside out! Knowing where to overtake, where to be careful, when to floor it and when to slow down in anticipation can make the difference between a place on the podium and being left long behind. The very best players also spend some time exploring all the shortcut options so they know whether they are worth taking or not!

RATING ★★★☆☆

← Aim for the boosts

The green boosters on the track are used by players to slingshot past rivals. However, for maximum advantage they need to be used properly. The top players learn where they are and get in track position early, rather than having to career from one side of the track to the other just to hit the boost – pulling off a difficult manoeuvre can negate the advantage of the speed boost!

RATING ★★★☆☆

→ Drive defensively

As players get close from behind, their profile pictures will appear at the bottom of the screen. This will alert players whether they are to their left or right, or directly behind them. Better players use this information to take up a track position that blocks any overtaking attempts, which is a useful tactic to employ!

RATING ★★★☆☆

← Dancing on the ceiling

Don't forget that the vehicles can attach their wheels to any flat surface. This can take a little getting used to, but is a brilliant way to get past obstacles – including other racers. Smart players can even use this approach to reach otherwise inaccessible speed boosts!

RATING ★★★★☆

THE THIRD PARTY ELIMINATION

THE PROBLEM:

Engaging opponents is always a risk because you may not be aware of their health, shield strength, or the weapons they possess. This becomes an even greater challenge later in the game when your surviving opponents are likely to be more skilled and experienced players.

OUR SOLUTION:

Listen (and look) out for combat near to you and find a safe vantage point. Wait for the players to fight each other and take advantage when there is only one (usually damaged) player left before making your move!

Step 1

The first rule of combat is a simple one – make sure you have a decent variety of weapons, that they are all loaded, and that you are in good health condition. There's no point in attacking anyone until you are ready for it.

Step 2

When you hear combat close by, move towards it quickly and find somewhere safe that lets you view the action without being seen – hiding in a bush, behind a wall or looking down on the action from above.

Step 3

Sit back and watch as your opponents duke it out. Keep a close eye on the battle – if one player appears to win quickly and easily without sustaining damage, it may be worth not getting involved after all.

Step 4

As soon as one player is eliminated, make your move. It can be worth pausing for just a second or so to see if the survivor makes life easy for you by stopping to heal up (an easy shot!) but if not, target them with ranged weapons.

Step 5

If possible, stay behind cover and shoot from a distance. If you must approach, move quickly and decisively to prevent enemies from hiding and healing.

Step 6

Once the survivor is eliminated, don't rush in to pick up the loot. Remember other players may be waiting to use the same trick on YOU. Take your time, use cover to get to the loot, and if it feels risky, leave it!

ZERO BUILD

Zero Build is growing in popularity all the time – many players like the way it levels the playing field by stopping the elite builders winning all the time. As a different game mode, it requires a specialist approach to certain situations – so it's a good job the GamesWarrior crew have been poring through all the available tactics to pick out the most useful ones!

I like to move it!

It's easy to get trapped by the storm when there is no option to build, or to come under fire and not be able to escape. Carrying something like shockwave grenades is a useful trick to avoid those scenarios.

GAMESWARRIOR'S VERDICT

We recommend reserving one inventory slot for items that can help with mobility.

Use what's there

Another way that players get round the lack of materials in Zero Build is to make the most of existing buildings, using them as bases to defend from or take cover in.

GAMESWARRIOR'S VERDICT

We advise sticking close to buildings or settlements wherever possible so you have somewhere sensible to take refuge if you come under attack.

Building in Zero Build

Even though it's not possible to build using materials in Zero Build mode, there are still some building options available. Some gamers prefer using a few instabuilds, like Portaforts, to quickly gain additional cover if they come under attack.

GAMESWARRIOR'S VERDICT

We suggest keeping a few in your inventory so that you can buy yourself valuable seconds if you do come under fire!

Look down on your opponents

In the absence of building, high ground becomes a much bigger advantage in Zero Build. Players who have high ground and fire down on their opponent are more likely to succeed as they can take a step back from the edge to take cover, while those lower down will have nowhere to hide.

GAMESWARRIOR'S VERDICT

We recommend avoiding initiating combat with players who are on higher ground than you unless it is unavoidable — always look for the high ground yourself.

Instant healing

Not being able to build means players are often at their most vulnerable when healing. Many players will hide in bushes or buildings to heal, but this tip is no good if players take damage in combat.

GAMESWARRIOR'S VERDICT

We suggest prioritising healing items that take instant effect and don't take ages to consume — fish or chug splashes, for example, rather than big pots or medkits.

41

Sneak up on opponents

Without the ability to build, starting combat from long range can be risky. It often just alerts the target to their attacker's location and gives them time to plot a counterattack.

GAMESWARRIOR'S VERDICT

We recommend using stealth and cunning to get as close as possible to an opponent before opening fire so that your shots are more likely to land.

Grab some wheels

Using vehicles is hugely important in Zero Build mode. Cars are a better option than motorbikes because they offer some degree of cover from incoming fire, and can also be used as cover once the journey is over. Vehicles can also be a useful way to drop from high areas without taking damage, as you can't build your way down.

GAMESWARRIOR'S VERDICT

We advise using cars for long journeys as you'll be vulnerable to sniper fire on foot!

A little helper

Hires are a big advantage in Zero Build — even more so in Solo mode. Most players find that a hire can distract opponents in combat too and use them to lead the way into new areas to prevent ambushes.

GAMESWARRIOR'S VERDICT

We suggest hiring supply or medic specialists as they will provide heals without making you hunt around for them — they'll bring the healing straight to you!

Allow your Overshield to recover

One of the big differences between traditional Battle Royale and Zero Build is the Overshield — an extra 50 hit points that can be sustained before the player's shield and health are impacted. The Overshield replenishes after a few seconds if it does take damage, even if health or the standard shield have been damaged.

GAMESWARRIOR'S VERDICT

We recommend staying behind cover until your Overshield is back to full strength if you come under fire, rather than rushing

Be aggressive

Zero Build mode offers greater rewards for aggression in combat than traditional Solo mode. The lack of an ability to build defensively means that damaged players often have nowhere to hide, so the better players attack more aggressively.

GAMESWARRIOR'S VERDICT

We think that following up an attack is a great way to stop your target's Overshield recovering, giving you the chance to drive home that advantage.

Burn brightly

In Zero Build, campfires are a valuable source of healing, and the best part is that they don't require any resources to use. However, players often forget about them because they don't have to collect wood.

GAMESWARRIOR'S VERDICT

We suggest keeping campfires in mind when you need healing, and moving around and crouching while using them to minimise the chance of getting hit.

Shhhh!

Unwanted noise is a major issue in Zero Build. With no chance to build defensively, no-one wants to let other players know where they are hiding.

GAMESWARRIOR'S VERDICT

That's why we advise looking out for silenced weapons whenever possible, or thrown explosives (like grenades) that won't give your position away!

Move and fire

In the early days of Fortnite, it was all about a victory dance after each elimination as players would rub their rival's nose in it. Those tactics are long gone, however.

GAMESWARRIOR'S VERDICT

We recommend being more cautious as other players may be attracted to the combat. Quickly take cover and avoid unnecessary risks.

THE DOUBLE RAMP

THE PROBLEM: You're confronted by a large obstacle between you and safety. It might be a large structure – more often it's a mountain with steep faces that are impossible to climb on your own. You need to build your way up to overcome the obstacle – but there may be snipers behind you waiting to pick you off as you do so.

OUR SOLUTION: Instead of building a simple single-layer ramp, you need to construct a two-level ramp. The lower level is to climb up. The upper level acts as a roof to the lower level, and provides you with cover from any eager snipers.

Step 1

Make sure you are far enough back from the obstacle that your ramp solution will make it to the top, rather than meeting the cliff face halfway up!

Step 2

Start with the roof level, building a double-width ramp immediately behind your avatar but angled towards the obstacle you want to climb over. You can do this by looking up and building.

Step 3

Build the first part of the ramp's 'floor' double-width so you can safely climb it before moving to the top.

Step 4

Look up to build another roof panel connected to the previous one, then down to build another floor panel to keep climbing.

Step 5

Keep repeating the process until you have reached the top of the mountain or building that was previously in your way! You can hold down your 'build ramp' button and simply alternate between looking up and down to build quicker.

Step 6

If you're low on building materials or in a hurry, you can build a single width ramp. However, this comes with a risk as it is easier for an enemy to shoot out the base of a narrow ramp, causing the whole thing to collapse.

GAMESWARRIOR'S VERDICT

Being able to reach higher areas without running the risk of being sniped from distance is a vital skill — once you master it, you'll be amazed how quickly it becomes second nature!

GW RATING ★★★★★

RANKED MODE EXPLAINED

The thrill of getting a Victory Royale is one thing, but if you want to compare your performance against other players over time, then Ranked mode tracks your performance and lets you do just that!

What is Ranked mode?

Ranked mode replaced the popular Arena game mode in Chapter 4 Season 3. The better you perform in ranked matches, the higher you can rise — play poorly, and you can drop again!

How the ranks work

The lower rankings all have three tiers, so you will work your way up through three levels each in Bronze, Silver, Gold, Platinum and Diamond. The highest levels — Elite, Champion and Unreal contain only one tier each. Once you reach Unreal, you can't be moved back down again — but you can be relegated from all other levels if you are eliminated early too often!

As you progress up through the rankings, you'll encounter players who have similar rankings to you, which means that the higher you go, the harder the games become.

Fortnite Rankings

Bronze 1,2,3
Silver 1,2,3
Gold 1,2,3
Platinum 1,2,3
Diamond 1,2,3
Elite
Champion
Unreal

Different modes for each game type

You will have different rankings for each game mode – Battle Royale and Zero Build. Being brilliant in Solo Zero Build won't impact your starting rank in Squads Battle Royale.

GAMESWARRIOR'S VERDICT

We believe that focusing your efforts on a single game mode is an effective way to get your rank as high as you can. So, pick the mode you play best in and devote your Ranked game time to it!

Stick together

The most successful players in Duos and Squads are the ones who frequently play alongside each other. By being familiar with their teammates' playing style, it becomes much easier for them to work together and advance through the game and secure a joint Victory Royale.

Gamers who are serious about securing a high ranking in Duos or Squads, play regularly with the same group of friends. By learning each other's playing style, they are likely to progress quickly together. However, playing Duos Fill in Ranked can be more challenging as the playing style of your teammate will change from game to game.

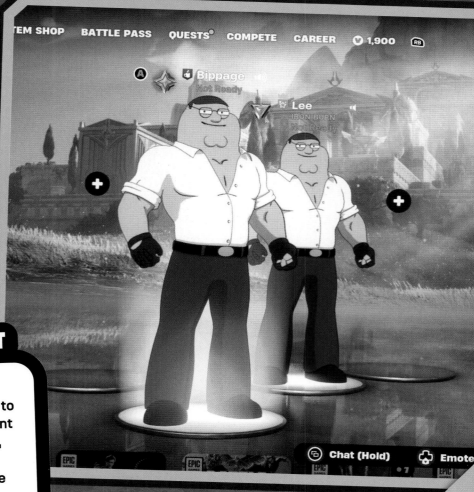

GAMESWARRIOR'S VERDICT

We think playing with the same friend or friends as often as you can is a great way to make quick progress. Playing with different partners all the time just confuses things, whereas if you try playing Duos Fill you might find that your teammate goes rogue and doesn't work with you at all.

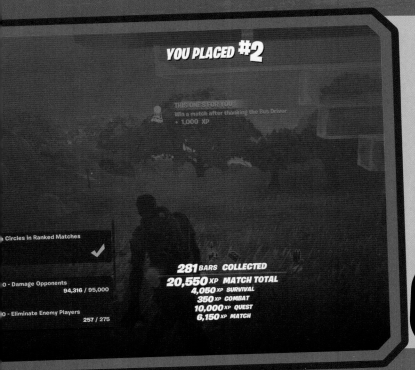

YOU PLACED #2

281 BARS COLLECTED
20,550 XP MATCH TOTAL
4,050 XP SURVIVAL
350 XP COMBAT
10,000 XP QUEST
6,150 XP MATCH

Don't dive straight in

Playing Ranked mode is not the best way to get familiar with a new season, a new area of the map or a new weapon. A poor start in Ranked mode means you'll have a far greater distance to climb. Players who've had lots of practise in Unranked games first know where to drop, places to avoid, how to use any new weapons effectively, and more.

GAMESWARRIOR'S VERDICT

In our experience, practising in Unranked games first is the best way to start out.

Use the host wisely

When playing Ranked Duos, the lobby will be based on the level of the lower-ranked player. If both players have similar levels, there is less of a risk of a mismatch. However, if the teammates are considerably different in ranks they will both level up a little quicker!

GAMESWARRIOR'S VERDICT

For this reason, we advise letting the lower-ranked player host, so that you are playing against lower-ranked opponents more often than not!

Hires

Securing yourself a hire in Ranked can be a major bonus. They'll help to take attention off of you, deal damage to opponents to help you finish them off quicker, and flush out enemies who are in cover.

GAMESWARRIOR'S VERDICT

We recommend hiring a helper to take risks so you don't have to — heading into buildings first, for example.

MANAGE TEAM MEMBER

IRON BURN

Ⓐ MAKE PARTY LEADER

WHISPER

KICK

VIEW PROFILE

MUTE

Ⓑ CLOSE

Scoring

The two biggest factors in your ranking score are your final position – how close you came to winning – and the number of eliminations you secured along the way. However, it's crucial to know that the two are linked, and that one is not much use without the other.

Eliminations are worth more points to your ranking when fewer players remain in the game. In other words, taking out an opponent when there are 90 players in the game is not as valuable as eliminating an opponent when only five players are remaining.

GAMESWARRIOR'S VERDICT

As a result, we advise concentrating on staying alive until the endgame and securing one or two late eliminations instead of being overly aggressive and risking an early elimination.

A common strategy some players adopt after landing and securing some weapons is to only initiate combat if they are sure they have the upper hand. Players who do not engage at all and stay out of sight for as long as possible can secure a higher finish.

Because the risk of an early exit is greater than the reward of securing some early eliminations, deciding where to land is extremely important. A long glide and a late drop can often see players in the top 85 before they've touched the ground!

GAMESWARRIOR'S VERDICT

We say avoid anywhere hot – look for quiet, out-of-the-way locations that are home to a reasonable amount of loot so you can gather a few weapons quickly, because those early skirmishes can be absolutely hectic!

GAMESWARRIOR'S VERDICT

We strongly advise a safety first approach when engaging with opponents. Firing wildly from a distance will only alert others to your presence. In fact, we find it's often best to adopt a stealth approach without firing for as long as you can if you want a high finish.

The GamesWarrior Way
USING VEHICLES

THE PROBLEM: The Island is a big place, especially when there are 99 rival players taking potshots at you! You need to move around quickly and efficiently, but at the same time you can't afford to draw unnecessary attention to yourself.

OUR SOLUTION: The best players use vehicles at the right time in the right way to give themselves the biggest possible advantage. We've investigated the best approaches to making the in-game vehicles work for you – here's what we suggest!

Step 1

Before you even get into a vehicle, it needs to be the right time to use one. Early on in the game, vehicles can be a great way to cover big distances – if you dropped somewhere too hot, for example. In a smaller storm circle, however, you need to consider the risk of alerting everyone to your location.

Step 2

Having decided to use a vehicle, try to find one that suits your needs – or at least use the vehicle you have in a way that suits it. Taking a sports car off road is a bad move, for example, as is driving a motorbike through a gun battle due to the lack of protection it offers.

Step 3

When using a vehicle, it's important to think ahead so you know where you're heading. Vehicles sink when they are driven through a large body of water, for example, so head round not through – and don't get caught at the foot of a sheer cliff!

Step 4

Your vehicle can be used as a weapon if the chance presents itself, mowing down any opponents who are in your path. It can be hard to do in normal play, but if they are distracted in a gun battle you have a great chance!

Step 5

Your vehicle can save you from damage as well as causing it to others! You can use it as cover, crouching alongside it, or use it to make huge drops that would otherwise cause you fall damage! Lastly, if you move into the passenger seat, the engine shuts off and you can hide!

Step 6

Once a vehicle is damaged enough, it will explode – so know when to say goodbye! Keep a eye on the damage meter and once your transport has around 25% health left, get out before it explodes and damages you!

The GamesWarrior
GUIDE TO WEAPON TYPES

If you want to be the last player standing, you'll need to know the key weapons inside out. While the exact options available change regularly, understanding what each basic weapon class is best at is a great place to start! Here's what we think about each weapon – including when to use them and when to avoid them!

Getting to know... shotguns

GamesWarrior likes

For inflicting lots of damage at close range, you can't beat a shotgun! You don't even have to be accurate as they spread their shot, meaning you will secure eliminations even without looking down the scope.

GamesWarrior doesn't like

Shotguns tend to have an absolutely tiny range, and will cause hardly any damage to opponents more than a few yards away. They can also be slow to reload which can leave you vulnerable!

When GamesWarrior doesn't use them...

If you're crossing open space or are in a situation where there's no chance of an opponent surprising you from close range, then a shotgun is as useful as a chocolate fireplace!

When GamesWarrior uses them...

Shotguns are brilliant in close quarters combat, especially when clearing a building or series of buildings. With a shotgun equipped, you'll be ready to handle any situation as you move from room to room.

Getting to know... submachine guns

GamesWarrior likes

The rapid-fire nature of a submachine gun (SMG) means that it can cause a lot of damage very quickly. They often come with large magazines – enough ammo to get the job done without reloading!

GamesWarrior doesn't like

That rapid-fire element can work against you. If you drift off target, you can waste all your bullets very quickly indeed!

GamesWarrior uses them...

SMGs are good at both close and medium distance, so they're ideal for crossing larger spaces like warehouses or courtyards, where a rival could appear at close range, but would never be too far away.

GamesWarrior doesn't use them...

Because they are no good at any kind of distance, SMGs are pointless when crossing open areas – if you're fired on from distance you'll have no chance of hitting back.

RATING ★★★★★

Getting to know... assault rifles

GamesWarrior likes

These are probably the most useful all-round weapon in the game. Their versatility means that as long as you have an AR in your inventory, you've got a good chance of winning most kinds of skirmish.

GamesWarrior doesn't like

Assault rifles are good at everything, but brilliant at nothing. At short range, shotguns are better. At close to mid range, you're better off with an SMG. At distance, grab a sniper rifle.

GamesWarrior doesn't use them...

At extreme distances, you need to find a sniper rifle rather than sticking with your trusty AR — and the same goes for close range combat — the AR doesn't do enough damage quickly enough to compete with an SMG or a shotgun!

GamesWarrior uses them...

Assault rifles are GamesWarrior's go-to weapon. Their versatility means they're ideal when you're heading into the unknown so we make them our usual carry, with specialist options for close-range and long-distance options tucked away in slots on either side.

GW RATING ★★★★★

Getting to know... sniper rifles

GamesWarrior likes

Sniper rifles are the only weapons capable of a one-shot elimination – a headshot will take a rival out instantly. Even a body shot can be enough to finish off a player with less than full shields.

GamesWarrior doesn't like

A sniper scope glints in the sun, so it can give your exact location away to any player who is looking in your general direction, so you can't use them to scan the horizon any more!

GamesWarrior doesn't use them...

Snipers should be avoided if any opponent is nearby. The scope makes them almost impossible to use at close quarters and the reload time between single shots is huge.

GamesWarrior uses them...

Sniper rifles are best used from cover, using the scope sparingly to avoid revealing your location to your target. They can also be used to scout out far-off locations to see if any opponents are lying in wait for you!

Getting to know... explosives

GamesWarrior doesn't like

You often can't carry many explosives in a single slot, so it's hard to launch a prolonged attack using them. They are also very loud and visible from a distance, so there's a chance you'll attract other players who might then cause you extra problems!

GamesWarrior likes

Explosives often don't give away your location – there's no sound when they are thrown, only when they land. They can also cause damage to a large area, meaning more than one opponent can be taken out in a single attack.

GamesWarrior uses them...

Explosives are great in team games, and can be particularly effective against squads hiding in one of their builds. A well-placed grenade or similar can damage or destroy the build as well as impacting on the whole squad while they hide.

GamesWarrior doesn't use them...

Your explosives can cause damage to you as well as your opponents, so they should not be used in tight, confined spaces. It's too risky that you'll hit a wall and they'll explode so close to you that you also suffer damage.

USING HIRES SUCCESSFULLY

THE PROBLEM: In a Battle Royale where it's every player for themselves, the odds are a bit too equal for our liking. Finding a way to get some extra help would be an excellent idea, wouldn't it?

OUR SOLUTION: The Island is home to non-playable characters (NPCs) that you can recruit to help. They each have different skills, but the extra firepower and support can make the difference between winning and losing!

Step 1

First up – hires cost money! They won't help you for free! To recruit them, you need to play smart when it comes to amassing plenty of gold. You might need to play a few games where you focus on generating revenue by raiding vaults or undertaking quests first.

Step 2

Different hires have different skills. Try to identify who you'd like to recruit and aim to land on them from the Battle Bus so that you maximise your advantage from the very start.

Step 3

Once your hire is on board, it's important to stay together. They'll respawn if you get too far from them, but try to avoid this – always wait for them to get into vehicles before driving off, for instance.

Step 4

Use the comms wheel to issue directions to your hire. For the most part, they should be set to follow you, but if you are playing stealthily, you should set them to hold position to avoid them opening fire on passing opponents.

Step 5

By setting a waypoint for your hire, you can order them to lead the way into battle. This is a great technique for distracting opponents or drawing them out from cover without risking damage to yourself!

Step 6

If you are playing multiplayer modes, don't forget you can order your hire to revive you if you get knocked! This means your human teammates can focus on dealing with the opponents that put you on the floor in the first place!

GAMESWARRIOR'S VERDICT

Using a hire almost always makes the game easier – using them properly gives you a far greater chance of success. They can distract opponents and help you eliminate them too – what's not to love?

RATING ★★★★★

Top 20
SUPER SKINS

With literally thousands of skins available, it's never been easier to look fabulous while going about your business on the Island! We've decided on our twenty favourite Fortnite skins, giving each one a rating out of five for how dope it looks, its celebrity status, and how well it camouflages the wearer. Do you agree with our countdown?

20

Midas
The gold-plated founder of Shadow and Ghost, this skin has an added bonus of turning every weapon he holds into gold (sadly it's just a cosmetic effect).

Dope: 5   Celeb: 1   Camo: 1

19

Agent Peely
Everyone's favourite six-foot banana cuts a dashing figure in a tuxedo!

Dope: 4   Celeb: 2   Camo: 1

18

Spire Assassin
A previous level 100 Battle Pass reward, Spire Assassin is definitely one of the coolest skins that money can't buy.

Dope: 5   Celeb: 1   Camo: 1

17

Cluck
A giant chicken that stands out from a mile away – Cluck is the ideal choice if you want to prove you're no chicken!

Dope: 5   Celeb: 1   Camo: 1

16

Agent Jonesy

Central to the Fortnite story, playing as Agent Jonesy shows you're a true games fan.

Dope: 5   **Celeb: 1**   **Camo: 2**

15

Plastic Patroller

An almost invisible skin when hiding in bushes and foliage, Plastic Patroller is a fantastic stealth outfit.

Dope: 2   **Celeb: 1**   **Camo: 5**

14

Meow Skulls

Here kitty kitty! There's nothing cute about this skin when Meow Skulls is bearing down on you. Are you feline lucky?

Dope: 5   **Celeb: 1**   **Camo: 2**

13

Fabio Sparklemane

Not everyone wants to blend in. If you want to stand out, then do it in style as a fabulous pink unicorn!

Dope: 5   **Celeb: 2**   **Camo: 1**

12

Doctor Slone

Another character from Fortnite's own story, Doctor Slone brings a touch of nerdy class to Fortnite!

Dope: 5   **Celeb: 1**   **Camo: 3**

11

J.B. Chimpanski

A chimpanzee test pilot is probably about as Fortnite as it gets. Check out his editable styles for an impressive wardrobe of options!

Dope: 5   **Celeb: 1**   **Camo: 3**

10

Peter Griffin

The Family Guy patriarch is still a hugely popular skin – partly for the comedy value of seeing Peter Griffin run, jump and climb!

Dope: 3   **Celeb: 5**   **Camo: 1**

9

Neymar Junior

One of the world's best footballers seems as at home with a shotgun in his hands as he does with a football at his feet!

Dope: 2   **Celeb: 5**   **Camo: 2**

8

8Ball Vs Scratch

Another Fortnite legend, 8Ball Vs Scratch is a great choice for skulking in the shadows!

Dope: 5   **Celeb: 1**   **Camo: 4**

7

Lando Calrissian

The coolest Star Wars character makes a very cool Fortnite skin. Just don't play cards with him.

Dope: 4   **Celeb: 4**   **Camo: 2**

6

Optimus Prime

His Fortnite skin is a little smaller than his on-screen presence – but he's no less impressive a sight!

Dope: 5   **Celeb: 4**   **Camo: 1**

5

Zeus

The Greek God rules over the Island with incredible power – and his regal looks cut a dashing figure in combat.

Dope: 5   **Celeb: 5**   **Camo: 1**

4

Predator

If ever a skin was destined to be right at home in the undergrowth, it's this one – sadly it doesn't have a cloaking function though!

Dope: 3 **Celeb: 4** **Camo: 5**

3

Indiana Jones

One of cinema's most intrepid adventurers looks perfectly at home in his new surroundings. Wonder if he has time to search for artefacts?

Dope: 5 **Celeb: 5** **Camo: 3**

2

Solid Snake

A true gaming god, the Solid Snake skin just oozes class and gaming heritage. It's a skin selection that lets everyone know that you know your gaming.

Dope: 4 **Celeb: 4** **Camo: 5**

1

Armored Batman Zero

I am the bat! Against a plethora of superhero skins, Armored Batman Zero manages to stand out as our favourite skin!

Dope: 4 **Celeb: 5** **Camo: 5**

TOP TEN GLIDERS

Arrive in style with a cool glider. There are hundreds to choose from, so we've selected our own top ten – do you agree with our choices?

10 Bombs Away

Rocking it old-school, fans of TNTina can ride a rocket all the way down to the ground – but this one won't explode on impact!

Woolly Mammoth

We love chonka tyres on vehicles, so why not arrive in style with this monster truck-themed glider?

9

8 Goalbound

If, like us, you love your footy, let the world know by gliding into the game using this soccer-tastic glider!

Skull-a-tron

Strike the fear of God into your opponents by arriving using this spooky – and very visible – skull glider.

7

6 Rick's UFO cruiser

Rick and Morty were certainly a big hit in their short time on the Island, so a Sanchez-inspired glider always goes down well.

5 Hadean Chariot

A more recent effort, this glider is inspired by the Greek Gods and sees you riding a chariot powered by demonic wild horses!

Salvaged chute

Lara Croft's glider will help you land on the Island unheard and possibly even unseen – a silent, unspectacular, stealthy way to start your Battle Royale!

4

3 Astroworld Cyclone

A badge of honour for those who were playing the game during Travis Scott's iconic Fortnite cameo, this is a glider that screams badass.

Millenium Falcon

Our favourite of the many Star Wars-inspired gliders, this glider even gives you a hyperspace-style effect when you deploy it!

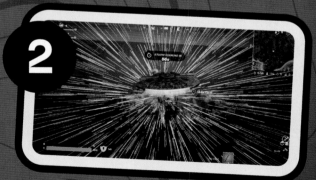

2

1 Victory Umbrellas

The victory glider changes each season, but once you've racked up your first Victory Royale, why not let everyone know that a winner is inbound to their game?

TOP TEN BACK BLINGS

Your skin choice isn't the only way to personalise your appearance in Fortnite – some well chosen back bling can help you create your own unique look! We've looked through hundreds of options to settle on this list of our top ten back blings – what's your favourite?

Fishstick Janky

The Fishstick Janky back bling is a quirky cosmetic. It's a dented fishstick, the same kind wielded by Fishstick himself. This floppy chrome fish adds a touch of humour and goes perfectly with fishy or aquatic skins!

Northquester Deluxe

This gold-trimmed satchel boasts a compass and map, hinting at adventures beyond the storm. Its sleek design, with red and black accents, speaks of refined taste. It can be a handy helper too, as the compass always points north, helping you orientate yourself as you move!

Pinata Brian

Forget sweeties, this piñata packs a punch (literally, it's Brian Griffin). This back bling Fortnite combines the Griffins' brainy dog with a loot llama. Candy cane stripes and a crow perched on his head complete the wacky design.

No Ghost

There's no better way to pay homage to the Ghostbusters than with this back bling. It proudly declares your affiliation with a glowing version of that famous logo. Be warned, however – it's visible from miles away and can help opponents spot you, especially in the dark!

Rocket

Groot's not-so-secret weapon hitches a ride! The Rocket back bling features Rocket Raccoon perched on your back, eyes peeled for trouble. This furry friend isn't just adorable, he's reactive! He perks up during combat and chills while gliding. While he might not blast enemies himself, Rocket adds a touch of personality to any outfit.

★★★★☆

Bobo

This mischievous monkey peeks out from your back, his eyes bulging wide with curiosity. With his manic expression, he looks like something from your worst nightmare, but love him or loath him, this little primate adds a playful touch to your spooky season style.

★★★★☆

Jones' Field Pack

This worn leather backpack holds everything an agent needs. A canteen and rolled-up map peek out, hinting at past missions, while a small piece of the zero point appears to be held in a container strapped to the side. Its simple design pairs well with any outfit, making it a versatile choice for the seasoned (or stylish) fighter.

★★★★☆

Pro-Adamantium Shield

Captain America's shield isn't just for defence! In Fortnite, it doubles as a sleek back bling. This vibranium beauty rests on your back, stars and stripes gleaming. Equip the matching pickaxe and watch the shield transform for harvesting duty. A true symbol of justice (and Victory Royale) for any hero.

★★★★☆

Neon Wings

Not your average angel wings. These bad boys crackle with electric energy, their vibrant colours pulsating in the night. Wearing this back bling is a clear statement of intent – you don't care who sees you, because you're good enough to take them down anyway. The very opposite of stealth!

★★★★★

Dimensional gate

The Dimensional Gate back bling is a portal to interdimensional power! This holographic backpack pulses with energy and hints at worlds beyond. Its cosmic design makes it a versatile accessory, pairing well with space-themed skins or standing out on its own.

★★★★★

TOP TEN HARVESTING TOOLS

There are lots of tools you can use to gather materials, and they are all as effective as each other. Your choices, then, come down to looks – so here are our ten favourite harvesting tools. What are yours?

Default Pickaxe

10

Simple things can be beautiful, perhaps best demonstrated by the simple elegance of the default pickaxe. Available to all, it will gather you just as many resources as its grander rivals – don't dismiss using it!

GW RATING ★★★★★

Vuvuzela

Responsible for one of the most annoying sounds to assault our ears from the stands of football stadia, the vuvuzela is far better suited to being bashed against trees and walls than trying to make 'music'.

GW RATING ★★★★★

9

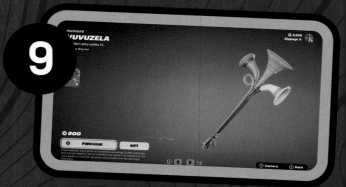

8

Pro-Adamantium Shield

One of the great things about using Cap's shield as a harvesting tool is that you don't need to be Captain America to use it! Though you can pair it with a Captain America skin and even have it as back bling as well!

GW RATING ★★★★★

Sludgehammer

The sludgehammer is a unique pickaxe with three styles in one. Originally a Battle Pass reward, it morphs between a pickaxe, an axe, and a sledgehammer. Part of the Slurp set, it even has selectable slurp juice colours!

GW RATING ★★★★★

7

Sigil of the Empire

The Sigil of the Empire pickaxe isn't for subtle harvesting. This Star Wars-themed Battle Pass reward gleams with the power of the dark side. Shaped like the Galactic Empire's crest, use it to channel your inner Vader!

★★★★☆ RATING

6

Bolt Blades

Charged with electric fury, the Bolt Blades crackles with power. These dual blades unleash the wrath of Zeus, their bright blue lightning design making them a standout cosmetic.

★★★★☆ RATING

5

Glownicorn Llamaxes

The Glownicorn Llamaxes pickaxe adds some whimsy to your harvesting. This sparkly unicorn pickaxe features a rainbow horn and a glowing mane, making it a vibrant addition to any locker.

★★★★★ RATING

4

Fret Basher

This electric guitar pickaxe lets you shred through structures with musical style, emitting musical notes with every swing. Fret Basher lets you express your inner rockstar and add some melody to the mayhem.

★★★★☆ RATING

3

Chainsaur

This dinosaur-looking chainsaw is not a quiet way to gather materials — everyone in earshot will know what you're up to! However, when you look this good doing it, who cares?!

★★★★☆ RATING

2

1

Mjolnir

This is perhaps the coolest of all the harvesting tools because it can only be wielded by Thor. Centuries of magical powers, and you get to use it to chop trees down for wood. What's not to love?

★★★★★ RATING

PLAYING STEALTHILY

THE PROBLEM:

The Island may seem a big place to start with, but the storm soon changes that and before you know it, you've got opponents all round you. The more obvious your presence is, the more likely you are to come under attack from multiple directions – you need to stay out of sight!

OUR SOLUTION:

Using stealth is a brilliant way to reach the later stages of games even if you aren't a particularly brilliant player. By selecting the right look, weapons and route, it's often possible to get to the last three or four players without even having to fire a shot!

Step 1

It all starts with sensible choices when it comes to your outfit. Dark, muted colours make hiding in shadows and bushes much easier. Go for greens and blacks, and avoid anything bright. Forget back bling and contrails too, and be sure to select a glider that doesn't make much noise – as well as a dull harvesting tool!

Step 2

When you walk or sprint, you make a noise. Other players will hear your footsteps (especially indoors where they can tell if you're a floor above them). To avoid giving your location away like this, crouch and walk slowly whenever possible – you'll often go completely unnoticed!

Step 3

Always be on the lookout for good places to hide. Bushes are a great start, as are dark shadows. Underneath staircases is a location many players don't pay attention to. Try to find places that offer some kind of cover too, so you can't be sniped or have an opponent sneak up behind you.

Step 4

Harvest sensibly so that you don't give your location away. Gather materials early when it's less likely there will be players near to you, and always look out for easy wins of materials lying on the floor. Harvesting walls from inside buildings is a great technique as it doesn't destroy your cover or cause trees to disappear, which can alert opponents to your location.

Step 5

Silenced weapons are kind when you're playing stealthily! Grab anything you can to keep your weapons quiet – modify them yourself if needed, and prioritise picking up quieter weapons when you find them. Keep a shotgun for close battle, but only as a last resort!

Step 6

If you want to stay out of trouble, plan your route carefully and watch the storm. By moving while you have time, you can skirt round open areas to stay in cover, for example. If you're sprinting from the storm you won't have that chance. Move early and use cover as you go.

LANDMARK
FOREST STATION

GAMESWARRIOR'S VERDICT

Even if you are normally an aggressive player, learning how to stay quiet and out of sight can be a crucial tactic when you're low on health, making stealth a vital skill to master!

GW RATING ★★★★★

BOOSTING XP QUICKLY!

Victory Royales are undoubtedly the ultimate measure of success in Fortnite – but even the best players in the world don't win EVERY time. The in-game ranking system sees players climb through different levels, even in 'unranked' matches. The currency used in the in-game levels is XP (experience points). The more XP a player earns, the quicker they will level up. We've looked at the best tactics to level up quickly – here's some of the best ways the pros do it!

Buy the Battle Pass

Buying the Battle Pass does cost V-Bucks but it usually unlocks a variety of Battle Pass-only challenges so all the top players make the purchase. However, as many mathematicians have pointed out, it isn't necessary to fork out money for the Battle Pass each season. Reaching level 100 will unlock enough V-Bucks in rewards to pay for the next Battle Pass. Considering all the skins you collect as part of the Battle Pass Journey, we think it's an approach that makes perfect sense!

RATING ★★★★☆

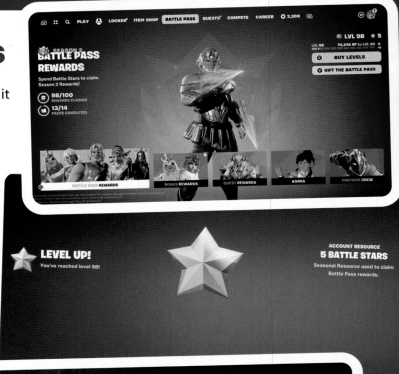

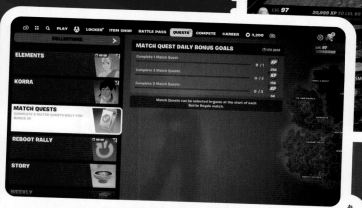

Daily challenges

Those players who reach the higher levels all have one thing in common – they play regularly. By logging on each day, it's possible to take advantage of the daily challenges every single day – if you only log on once a week, you will miss out on those challenges as they will not be saved. If you're serious about levelling up and gathering as much XP as possible, then hitting the daily challenges as many days as possible is definitely the way to go in our opinion.

GW RATING ★★★★☆

Know the challenges ahead

The players you encounter with crazy high ratings didn't get there by accident – they go out of their way to know what challenges are available to them at any point, and they keep an eye out for the opportunity to pick up extra XP within the game. For instance, they'll know that they are close to a reward for a certain number of eliminations using an assault rifle – so if they see the chance to finish an opponent off using one, they will.

We think it is a good idea to keep track of which challenges you are close to completing so you can look out for easy ways to bag some extra XP while you play. You can even choose to track a specific challenge you might be close to completing which will display on your HUD and serve as a reminder.

GW RATING ★★★☆☆

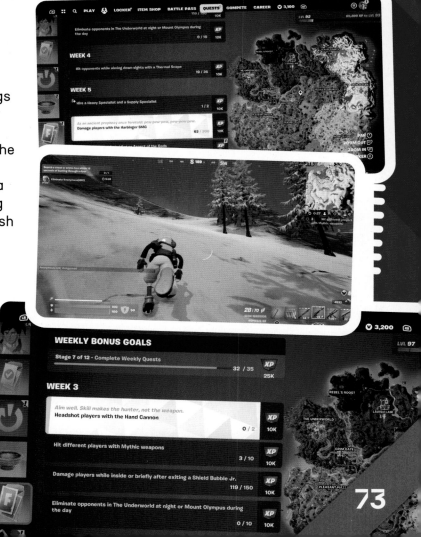

Laser focus

Some challenges are very specific and are unlikely to be achieved naturally by someone simply playing the game. They might include travelling from one location to another in a vehicle, for example, or holding three specific weapons simultaneously. The players that get these achievements ticked often set themselves the objective of completing the challenge first and only once it is done will they consider how they progress from there to trying to win the match.

Obviously, such an approach isn't for everyone – if you're the kind of player that takes their win ratio very seriously indeed, it won't appeal. If you are happy to spend a few games doing something a bit different, however, this is a great option. We find these challenges can also help you become a better player, as you might visit parts of the map you would ordinarily avoid, improving your knowledge of the Island in the process!

Team Rumble

Perhaps the most cunning of all the different tactics we've seen to boost XP points is those players who use Team Rumble to effectively farm XP. The games last so long and feature infinite respawns (as opposed to Battle Royale's return to lobby every time you're eliminated) so it's much easier to really rack up lots and lots of points. It's also a good environment to undertake longer challenges (completing a race track in a set time, for example) as sometimes they'll be set a long way from the action so you can complete them relatively undisturbed. When it comes to grinding out lots and lots of XP in the quickest time possible, we don't think playing Team Rumble can be beaten.

Playing the game

It's a simple option and it's staring you in the face, but don't forget that you gain XP in the game just by doing normal things. Opening crates, eliminating opponents and so on all result in XP, and simply playing the game can help keep your XP bar rising. We recommend keeping that in mind and opening as many crates and chests as you can. Many players with a full ammo bar would leave an ammo crate unopened, but we say open it anyway and take the 100XP – it all adds up! This isn't a tactic that will boost your XP super quickly, but it still helps on that journey and over lots of games, it can add up to a few levels!

Seize the moment

Sometimes there are limited time events in the game, and the smarter XP players will make the most of those opportunities. It might be that visiting a party mode (such as Coachella) or playing a new mode (such as Lego) brings an immediate and easy XP reward. Alternatively, it might be that a character is on the Island for a short time – for example, when Star Wars joins the party each year. When that happens, it is a smart plan to prioritise ticking off those short-term XP opportunities quickly, before they disappear for good!

LEGO FORTNITE

It's a match made in heaven — the creative freedom and genius of Lego joined with the cultural and gaming phenomenon that is Fortnite. However, Fortnite's foray into the Lego universe is much more than a cosmetic makeover; it's a fully-fledged creative playground known as Lego Islands.

This isn't just one mode, but a series of ever-expanding experiences that capture the pure joy of Lego building and imaginative play with a distinctly Fortnite flavour. Here's why Lego Islands is a blast for players of all ages.

Bringing buildings to life

The core of Lego's appeal is the freedom to create, and Lego Islands translates that brilliantly. Unlike the traditional Fortnite map, here you can smash apart pre-built structures and rebuild them into anything your imagination desires. Want a towering pirate ship? A sprawling medieval castle? With a vast library of Lego bricks at your disposal, the possibilities are endless! This isn't just about aesthetics; your creations can serve a purpose. Build bridges to traverse chasms, elaborate traps to outsmart enemies, or simply a cosy base to call your own!

LEGO BATTLE ARENA
53s 4/6 WAITING FOR PLAYERS

Themed adventures

Lego Islands aren't just sandbox experiences. Each Island boasts a unique theme, like the swashbuckling Lego Raft Survival. Here, you and your friends team up to build a sturdy raft, gather resources, and battle the legendary Blackbeard and his crew. Another exciting mode, Lego Obby Fun, throws you into a delightful obstacle course designed by real Lego designers. With over 300 levels to conquer, it's a fantastic test of your platforming skills and teamwork.

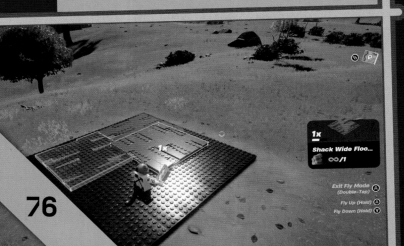

Lots to do

While construction is king, Lego Islands offers a delightful mix of activities. Explore vibrant worlds teeming with secrets and hidden collectables, solve puzzles that challenge your logic and ingenuity, and team up with friends to take down enemy AI or compete in friendly challenges. The variety ensures there's always something new to discover, keeping gameplay fresh and engaging.

Adaptability is the essence of true skill.

BRITE BOMBER

Aaah! What have I told you about sneaking up on me when I'm building?!

Continue

TyThom24

HEAVE HO!
MintElliot

9,400

Constant evolution

The beauty of Lego Islands is that it's constantly evolving. It isn't just about replicating the Fortnite experience with a Lego skin. It's a celebration of creativity, exploration, and the pure joy of building something amazing. So, grab your friends, unleash your imagination, and dive into the ever-expanding world of Lego Islands - you won't be disappointed.

A welcoming world

Lego Fortnite game modes prioritise fun and creativity over intense competition. The atmosphere is lighthearted and family-friendly, making it a perfect space for players of all ages and skill levels. Whether you're a seasoned Fortnite veteran or a newcomer to the world of building blocks, Lego Islands welcomes you with open arms.

GAMESWARRIOR'S VERDICT

In a game that constantly adds new adventures, game types and franchises into the mix, Lego is possibly the best Fortnite expansion to date. Great fun for all the family, and well worth a look (however old you are!).

GW RATING ★★★★★

CHALLENGE ANSWERS

How did you do? **Is your Fortnite fan status legendary?**

Crossword answers

Down
1 Royale
2 Sniper
3 Lego
4 Team Rumble
6 Shotgun
7 Chest
11 Squads
12 Slurp

Across
5 Harvesting
8 Grenade
9 Battle Bus
10 V Bucks
13 Glider
14 Llama

Wordsearch answers